NEKANE. THE LAMIÑA & THE BEAR

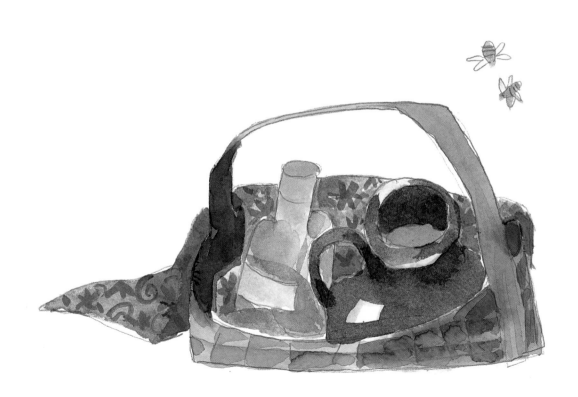

Rayve Productions Inc.
Box 726 Windsor CA 95492 USA

Publisher's Cataloging in Publication:
 Araujo, Frank P.   Nekane, the lamina & the bear: a tale of the Basque Pyrenees /
 by Frank P. Araujo; illustrations by Xiao Jun Li.
  p. cm. -- (Toucan tales)
 **SUMMARY: Retelling of a Basque folktale that pits a quick-witted
 young heroine, Nekane, against a mysterious foe, the lamina.**
 ISBN 1-877810-01-0
 1. Folk literature, Basque--Juvenile literature. I. Li, Xiao Jun, ill.   II. Title.   III. Series.
 GR137.7.A73 1993   398.2'04999'2   QBI93-760
 Library of Congress Catalog Card Number 93-84620

NEKANE, THE LAMIÑA & THE BEAR

A Tale of the Basque Pyrenees

by Frank P. Araujo, PhD
illustrations by Xiao Jun Li

Long ago, a little Basque girl named Nekane (*pronounced Ne-KAH-nay*) lived in a fishing village at the foot of the Pyrenees Mountains between present-day Spain and France. One summer day her mother called her and said, "Nekane, take this basket of fish and olive oil to your Uncle Kepa. Since you have to go through the woods, beware of the *lamiña* (the forest spirit). It loves olive oil and will try to get it by taking some shape, living or not."

"*Bai, Ama* (Yes, Mother). But how can I know the lamiña?"

"Remember, it is limited by the form it takes. If it becomes a bird, it can fly but it can't breath underwater like a fish. Also, it doesn't like dogs or fires in hearths. And it will never let you see its feet. So be sure to keep your wits about you."

"I will be very careful." Nekane replied.

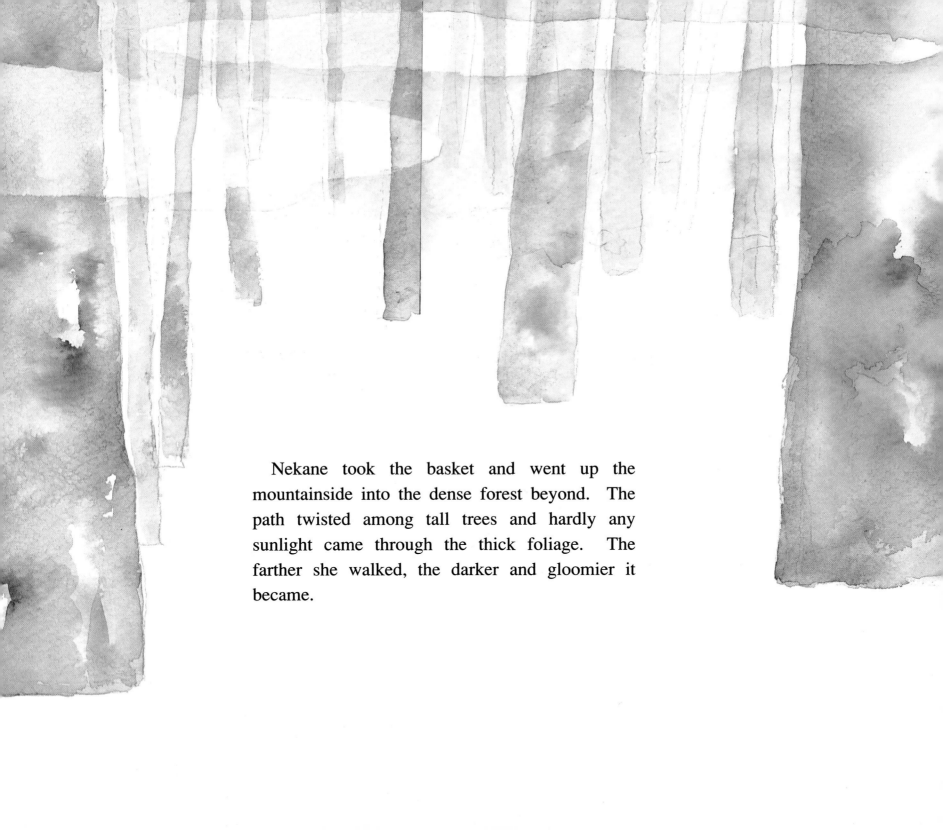

Nekane took the basket and went up the mountainside into the dense forest beyond. The path twisted among tall trees and hardly any sunlight came through the thick foliage. The farther she walked, the darker and gloomier it became.

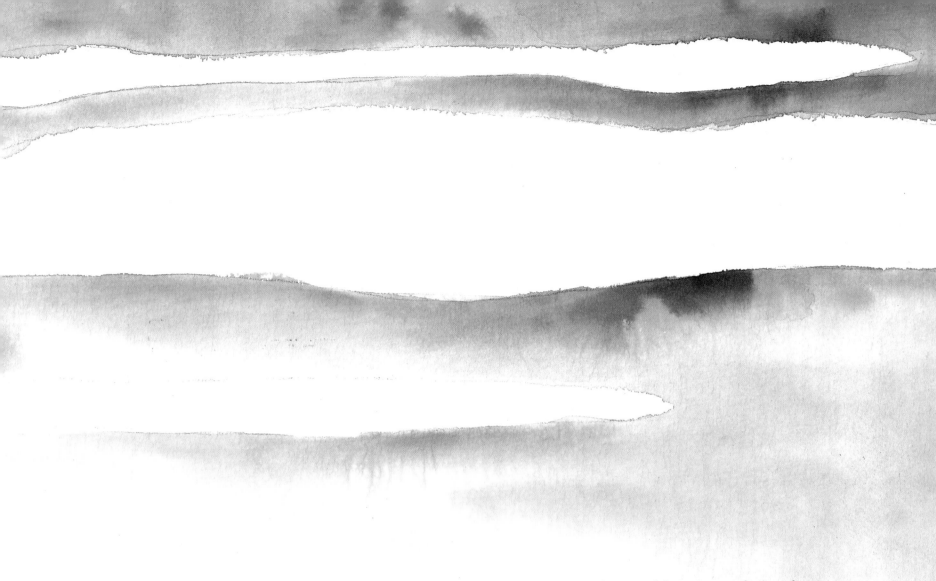

Suddenly, thick fog swirled around Nekane. It was so dense she could not see the path. Then unseen hands tugged at her basket as a ghostly voice spoke from the fog.

"*Neska tipia* (little girl), you will get lost in the fog."

The lamiña! And it wants my olive oil, Nekane thought, holding the basket tightly.

"Leave your basket and go on," said the voice.

"*Ez* (No)! You will leave me here in this terrible fog," Nekane cried.

"I **am** the fog. Give me the olive oil. When I have it, I will go away," spoke the ghostly voice.

"I don't believe you," said Nekane. "Before I do anything, show me the end of the path."

"Oh, very well," the voice said impatiently.

The fog parted and seeing the clearing a short distance in front of her, Nekane bolted and ran as fast as she could. With a gurgled cry, the fog closed but Nekane reached the clearing. There in the sunlight, Nekane felt a strong breeze blow down from the mountain.

"Now you'll be blown away because of the shape you have taken," she cried.

"You tricked me," the voice sighed and drifted back into the woods.

Relieved but uneasy about her escape, Nekane watched the fog retreat.

Nekane crossed into the part of the forest where her Uncle Kepa lived. The sun had come out and she skipped along the path in cheery sunlight. Then, as she came around a bend in the path, she heard a low growl. There in front of her was a huge bear.

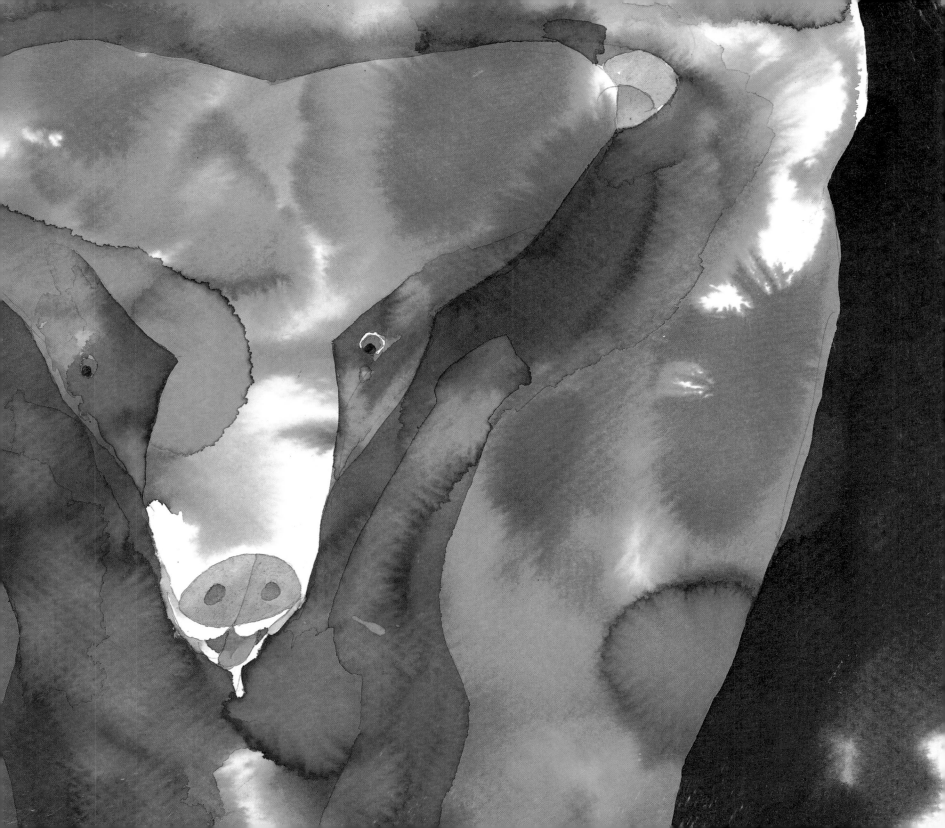

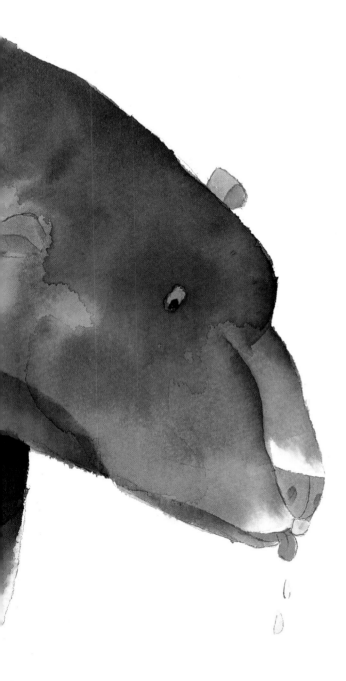

Is this the lamiña again? wondered Nekane. *No, I can clearly see his paws.*

The bear said, "You and the fish in your basket will be my dinner."

Nekane quickly answered, "*Oh, Hartz Jauna* (Mr. Bear), I'm much too small for your dinner. Besides, if you eat me and my few fish, you'll lose the chance to eat *ezti asko* (lots of honey)."

"*Ezti asko!* Where?" said the bear, beginning to drool.

"My Uncle Kepa keeps bees and will give you all the honey you can hold if you don't eat me."

"Hmm. I don't trust humans," said the bear, "but I do love honey. Very well. Take me to your Uncle's. But I'd better get the honey!"

As they went along, Nekane whispered to herself. "How can I warn Uncle Kepa? I can't outrun the bear. What will I do?"

With the bear close beside her, Nekane climbed the mountain to her uncle's place. When they came in sight of the house, the bear said, "Wait! The man with the sheep lives here. I know about him and his dog. I'll hide in these bushes, but if you don't bring me the honey, I'll come in and eat you both. Dog or no dog."

The bear crouched in the bushes while Nekane went up to the door.

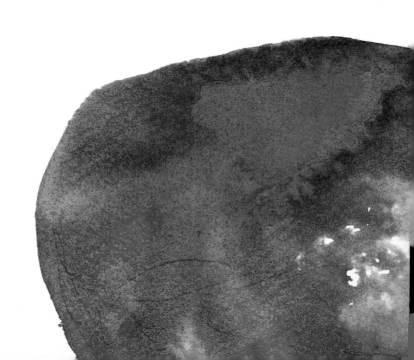

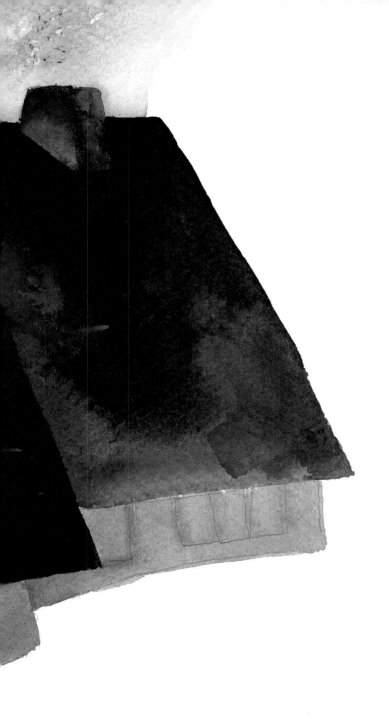

I do hope Uncle Kepa is home, she thought and then called, "Uncle Kepa, Uncle Kepa! It's Nekane."

"Come in, Nekane," said a voice from inside.

Nekane walked into a cold, dark house. Her uncle stood back in the shadows and did not even give her a hug!

"Uncle Kepa, there's a . . ."

"Yes, Nekane. Give me your basket," he said.

"But, Uncle Kepa..."

"Never mind. Just give me the basket," came his sharp reply.

Nekane was astonished. *Why won't Uncle Kepa let me tell about the bear?* And looking around she thought, *Where's his dog?*

"Uncle Kepa, where is Xotto?" she asked.

"What?"

"Where is Xotto, your dog?"

"Oh, he's out chasing rabbits."

Now Nekane knew something was wrong. Xotto never left her uncle's side; and herd dogs are not allowed to chase rabbits. Then she noticed that Uncle Kepa's feet were hidden in the shadows. *The lamiña!* she thought and said aloud, "Uncle Kepa, you have a hole in your shoe."

"What?" The false Uncle Kepa screamed. "Enough nonsense. Give me that basket."

Nekane darted out the door with the lamiña right behind her shouting for the basket. She raced to the bushes where the bear was hiding.

"*Hartz Jauna*, Mr. Bear. Uncle Kepa is here to give you the honey."

With a lick of his chops, the bear stood up and stuck his nose in the face of the false Uncle Kepa.

"Human, give me the honey or I'll eat you like a berry."

"Go away," the lamiña said. "Don't be fooled by this clothing. I'm not a human, and I don't have any honey."

"I've been tricked!" snarled the bear and started for the lamiña.

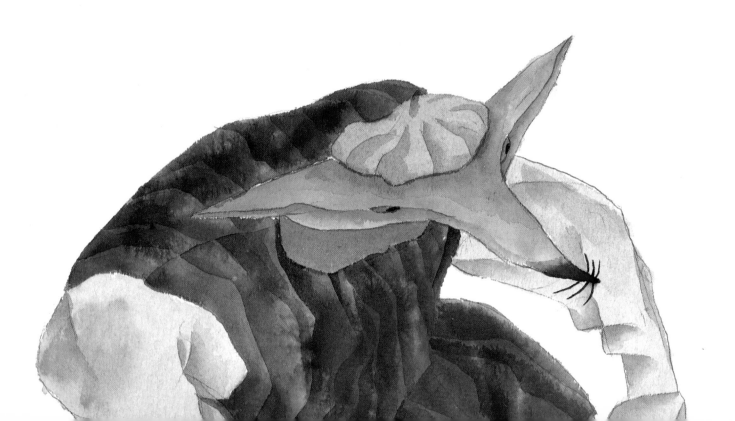

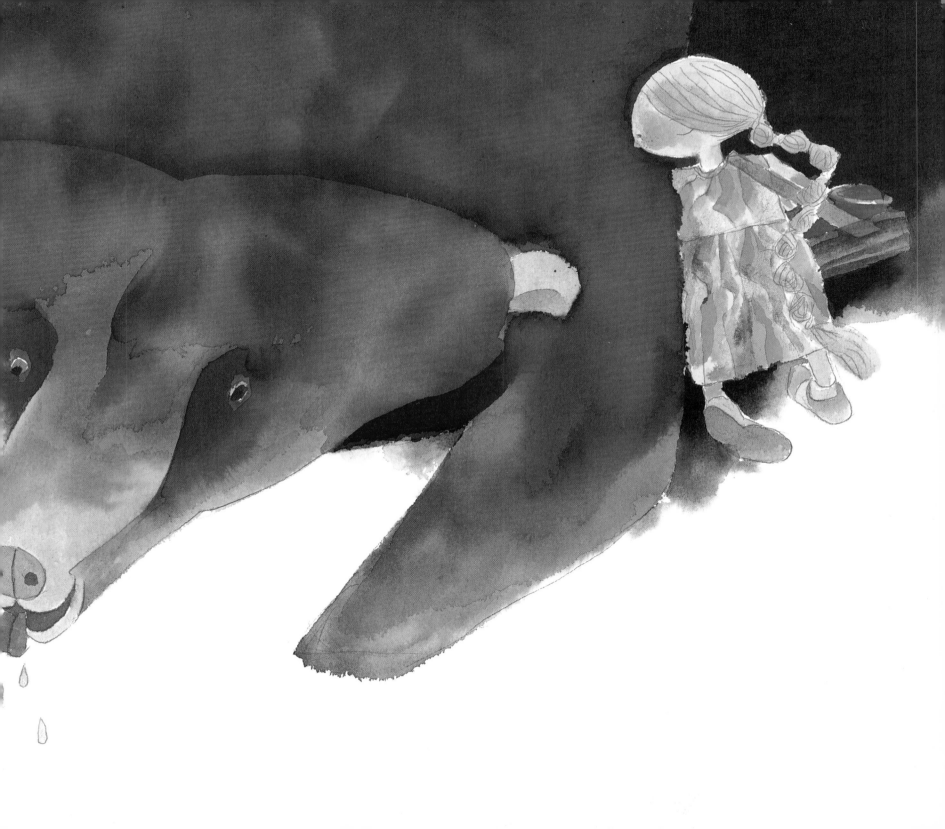

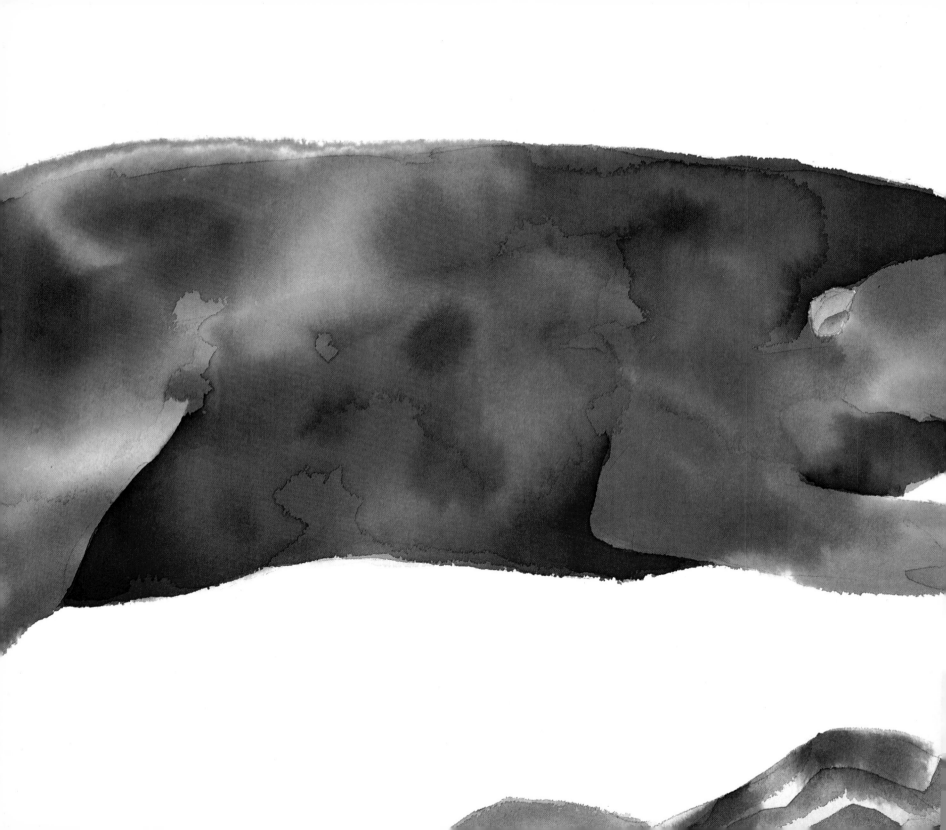

The lamiña stepped back and with a whoosh, the clothing flew off.

"See, you silly bear. I told you I'm not a human."

"I hate foxes more than humans!" The bear snarled, "Now, I'll eat you—bushy tail and all!"

Down the trail the bear chased the lamiña, who kept shouting, "I'm not really a fox" and struggled to keep his long, bushy tail from the bear's snapping teeth. Nekane watched them until they disappeared over the hill.

"Nekane, what joy!" spoke a familiar voice. Uncle Kepa had returned home with the sheep. Xotto bounded up to Nekane, barking and wagging his stub of a tail. Uncle Kepa picked her up, gave her a big hug, and kissed her on both cheeks.

"I brought you some olive oil and fish," Nekane said.

"And you brought me **you**. That's more wonderful than any old olive oil and fish. Come, have some bread and honey. And you can tell me the latest news.

"*Bai-to, osaba* (Well now, uncle)," said Nekane. "Do I have a story to tell!"

A GLOSSARY OF BASQUE TERMS

ama: Mother [pronounced **ah-ma**]

bai: Yes [pronounced **bye**]

bai-to: Well, now [pronounced **bye-toe**]

Basque: [pronounced **Bask**] The name of an ethnic group living in the Western Pyrenees Mountains and adjacent Atlantic coastal areas of Northern Spain and Southwestern France. The Basques have lived in that region since the Stone Age and speak a language that is unrelated to any other of the world's languages. They are well known throughout the Western United States for their role in the American sheep industry.

ez: No [pronounced **ess**]

ezti asko: Lots of Honey [pronounced: **ess-tee ahsh-koh**]

hartz: Bear [pronounced: **hahrts**]

jauna: Lord, Mister [pronounced: **yow-UN-ah**]

lamiña: Mischievous forest spirit [pronounced: **la-MEEN-ya**]

Nekane: A girl's name [pronounced: **Ne-KAH-nay**]

neska: Girl [pronounced: **nesh-ka**]

osaba: Uncle [pronounced: **oh-SHA-ba**]

tipia: Little [pronounced: **tee-PEE-ya**]

Xotto: Fred, a dog's name. [pronounced: **SHO-tso**]